GIANT
Dance Party

By

BETSY BIRD

ILLUSTRATED BY

BRANDON DORMAN

Greenwillow Books

An Imprint of HarperCollinsPublishers

For Matt. The first one goes to you, and for the best of reasons—B. B.

For Ellie Mae, you make our hearts dance each and every day—B. D.

Library of Congress Cataloging-in-Publication Data: Bird, Betsy. Giant dance party / by Betsy Bird ; illustrated by Brandon Dorman.
p. cm. "Greenwillow Books." Summary: Six-year-old Lexy Tanz loves dancing so much that she wants to share her skills with others, and when she is becoming discouraged because no one wants lessons from a girl so small, a herd of hairy giants arrives to test her teaching ability.
ISBN 978-0-06-196083-3 (trade bdg.) [1. Dance—Fiction. 2. Giants—Fiction.] I. Dorman, Brandon, ill. II. Title.
PZ7.B5118798Gi 2013   [E]—dc22   2011002492
13 14 15 16 SCP 10 9 8 7 6 5 4 3 2 1 First Edition   Greenwillow Books

The sign held up reads:

I Quit Ballet!
and tap and jaz
and tango and
Scottish Highland
dancing!

One day Lexy decided that when it came to dancing,
she was done.

"What about swing?" asked her mom.

Lexy held up her sign.

Her parents couldn't understand it.

"But, Lexy, you love to dance,"
said Mom.

"You *live* to dance,"
added Dad.

"I do. I do love dancing,"
Lexy admitted. "But I'm done!"

Her parents exchanged a look.
They knew why.
Those recitals.

Lexy loved dancing at home, you see.
She loved dancing with her friends.

What she did *not* love was dancing in a show. When the curtains opened, Lexy would step onto the stage, desperately wanting to dance. But all those eyes in the audience would look right at her, and she would forget to breathe. Then she'd freeze like an ice pop and never dance a step. Not one. Not ever.

So she tried
hypnotism.

She tried pretending
Moore and Carroll and
Anne were people.

She practiced for her parents
every night while they tried
to watch TV.

And every time she was sure her stage
fright was gone, along came another
recital, and *blammo!* Ice pop.

Then it hit her.

The perfect plan.

"I know, I know, I know! I'll be a dance *teacher*!" she cried.

Oh, the minute she said it, she knew it was a great idea.

Teachers never have to perform.

No stages. No shows. No audience. No ice pops.

Just dancing all day, every day.

Lexy got busy. On Monday, she made posters and taped them
on all the telephone poles in her neighborhood. Then she went
home and waited for her students to start lining up.
Nobody came.

On Tuesday, she pushed all
the furniture in the living room
out of the way.
Nobody came.

On Wednesday, she blasted
snap-happy mambo music
from the porch.
Nobody came.

On Thursday, she stared out
the window for five hours
without so much as a blink.
Nobody came.

On Friday, she gave up. No one wants to learn from a kid, she thought gloomily. Especially not a kid who's afraid of dancing in front of an audience.

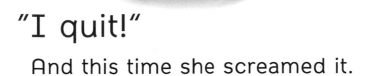

"I quit!"

And this time she screamed it.

Then, on Saturday, somebody came.

Now, let's be clear about one thing. Giants? Yeah, they don't dance. They stumble and they stomp and they stretch and scratch, but that's not exactly dancing. That's why it was so weird when five of them showed up at Lexy's house on Saturday morning and bellowed, "DANCE LESSONS, PLEASE!"

"Go away!" she replied.

She couldn't teach giants! They were too big.

And furry. And blue. She made little shooing motions

with her hands. "Go away!"

The giants didn't move.

"Uh . . . I quit yesterday," she tried.
The giants folded their arms, crossed their legs,
and sat down. They stuck out their lower lips.
Birds perched on them.
"Why do you want to learn to dance,
anyway?" she eventually said.

"We love to dance!" said the biggest one.

"We live to dance!" agreed the others.

"But nobody will teach us *how* to dance,"
said one of the smaller giants.

A giant stuck Lexy's poster under her nose
and gave her a little smile.

Lexy blinked. She looked down
at her poster. It *did say* she would
teach anyone.

"Well . . . okay," she said quietly,
though honestly she didn't know
where to start.

The giants didn't notice. They just
gave one another high fives
and bounced with glee.

The next part wasn't easy. The giants weren't kidding when they said they didn't know how to dance.
But Lexy turned out to be a good teacher. She showed the giants how stumbles were steps, stomps were taps, and stretches could turn into cool disco moves. She even demonstrated how scratches could morph into jazz hands.

Next, she gave each giant a dance to work on.

Gully:

Irish Step Dancing

Neesha:

The Twist

MacDuff: Interpretive Dance

Molina:

Krumping

Polly:

The Chicken Dance

They practiced. They studied. Then they practiced some more. Then they pranced and spun and leaped and twirled.

Before long, they were ready. It was time to show the world. It was time for a giant dance recital.

Lexy and Polly and Molina and MacDuff and Neesha and Gully got busy. They worked on costumes, selected their music, and taped posters all over town. Everyone planned to come. Giants dancing? Seriously? Who would miss that?

GIANT DANCE RECITAL

When the big night arrived, Lexy felt the familiar butterflies in her stomach. At least *she* wouldn't have to dance. Instead she gave her giants a big smile, patted them on the heels, and said, "You can do it!" You could hear their knees knock as they stepped onto the stage.

Uh-oh.

The music started.

The audience waited.

Not a single giant moved.

Not one.

They just stood there

like gigantic furry blue ice pops.

Question: How do you warm up frozen giants?

Answer: You dance!

Lexy didn't think. She danced. She leaped onto the stage
and did cancans and pirouettes. A break-dancing spin,
an electric slide, and a Shuffle Off to Buffalo.

MacDuff was the first to see her leaping.
So he swayed. Just a little. MacDuff moved
to his own beat.

Neesha noticed next.
She tapped a toe and
twisted herself into circles.

Polly's chicken dance was
elegant and refined.

The music picked up. The giants got bouncier.
And bouncier.

Gully's toes pounded
the stage till it shook.

Molina moved so fast
it was like watching fur fly.

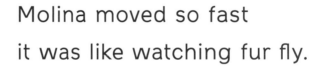

And the audience laughed and cheered and
threw bouquets of flowers. What a show!
What a performance! What a giant dance party!

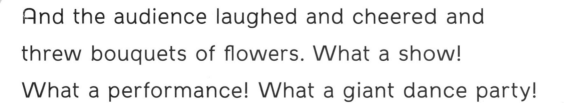

The giants took their bows with pride. And as they drew Lexy out for a final encore, she beamed. Her fears were long gone. She may not have been a giant but, boy, did she feel big.

Of course, that didn't mean she wasn't
still scared of *other* things.

Reading aloud in class was tough.

Playing sports was agony.

And as for singing. . . .